PADDINGTON AT THE SEASIDE

For older children Michael Bond has
written ten Paddington storybooks,
all illustrated by Peggy Fortnum.

CIP data may be found at the end of the book.

Paddington
at the Seaside

MICHAEL BOND & FRED BANBERY

RANDOM HOUSE
New York

First American Edition 1978. Text Copyright © 1975 by Michael Bond.
Illustrations Copyright © 1975 by Fred Banbery and William Collins Sons & Co., Ltd.
All rights reserved under International and Pan-American Copyright Conventions.
Published in the United States by Random House, Inc., New York.
Originally published in Great Britain by William Collins Sons & Co., Ltd., London.
Manufactured in the United States of America   1 2 3 4 5 6 7 8 9 0

"Today," said Mr. Brown at breakfast one bright summer morning, "feels like the kind of day for taking a young bear to the seaside. Hands up, all those who agree."

Jonathan, Judy, and Mrs. Brown all put up their hands.

And Paddington raised both of his paws as well, just to make sure.

Everyone was very excited, and by the time they set out the Browns' car was so full of things there was scarcely room to move.

Paddington carefully fastened his seat belt,
and then peered out of the window as he felt
the car turn a corner.

"Are we nearly there, Mr. Brown?" he asked
hopefully.

Mr. Brown removed a shovel handle from his
left ear. "I'm afraid not," he said gloomily.
"We've only just left Windsor Gardens, and it's
a very long way to the sea."

Mr. Brown was right. It *was* a long journey. But when they reached the seaside the sight of the sand and the water soon made up for it.

Paddington gave an excited sniff as he climbed out of the car. Even the air had a different smell.

"That's because it's special seaside air," said Mrs. Brown. "It's very good for you."

Paddington looked around anxiously as
Mr. Brown began laying out the beach things.

"I hope all the air doesn't get used up, Mrs.
Brown," he said in a loud voice. And he gave a
man who was doing some deep-breathing
exercises a very hard stare indeed.

"Come on, Paddington," called Judy. "Let's go for a swim."

It took Paddington a while to get ready. He wasn't the sort of bear who believed in taking chances, and by the time he went into the sea he was wearing so many things he promptly sank.

"No wonder!" cried Judy, as she went to his rescue. "You haven't even bothered to blow up your paw-bands!"

"Fancy wearing a duffle coat!" exclaimed Jonathan.

"I thought the water might be cold," gasped Paddington.

After his paw-bands had been properly blown up, Paddington went in the water again. And with some help from Jonathan and Judy he was soon swimming very well indeed.

After his swim Paddington settled down in
a deck chair in order to dry out.

He had barely closed his eyes when he heard
something very strange going on behind him.

First there was a loud cry.

Then there was the sound of people booing.

"They're watching Mr. Briggs' Punch and
Judy," explained Mrs. Brown.

Paddington jumped up and looked at the others as if he could hardly believe his ears. But Mr. and Mrs. Brown seemed much too busy with the picnic things to be bothered, so he turned and hurried up the beach towards the spot where the noise was coming from.

"Where's Paddington?" asked Jonathan, when he and Judy arrived back shortly afterwards carrying ice-cream cones and an ice stick.

"I hope he's not long," said Judy. "I brought him a special giant cone. He'll be most upset if it all melts."

Jonathan glanced up and down the beach. "Crikey!" he said suddenly. "Look over there!"

The Browns gave a gasp as they turned to
follow the direction of Jonathan's gaze.
Something very odd seemed to be going on
inside the Punch and Judy tent.

There was a large bulge in one side and it was
heaving up and down almost as if it were alive.

Suddenly the tent began moving across the sand, scattering people in all directions. It just missed a large sand castle, went twice around the ice-cream man, and then headed towards the sea.

"Quick!" shouted Judy. "Let's cut it off!"

But she was too late.

"Paddington!" cried Judy, as a familiar figure swam into view. "What on earth are you doing? That's the second time I've had to rescue you!"

Paddington stared at her in amazement. "But I went to rescue *you*!" he exclaimed. "Mrs. Brown said you were being punched by Mr. Briggs."

Mrs. Brown looked at Paddington in astonishment. Then her face cleared.

"I didn't say Mr. Briggs was *punching* Judy," she explained. "I said it was his Punch *and* Judy."

"It's a puppet theater," said Judy. "They often
have them at the seaside. There's one puppet
called Mr. Punch, and when he gets cross all the
audience have to boo."